# Wonderf
# Marvelously
# Brown

written by
## XOCHITL DIXON

WATERBROOK

illustrated by
## SARA PALACIOS

Dazzling, glorious,
spectacular **brown**
is the color of people
I see in my town.

Everywhere that I go
I'm searching to see
something **wonderfully,**
**marvelously brown**
—just like **me!**

**Brown** like new school desks.
Corkboards covered with tacks.
Brown like paper-sack lunches
stuffed with lip-smacking snacks.

**Brown** like freckles and moles
and birthmarks on faces.
Brown like teachers with maps
for exploring new places.

**Brown** like white-throated sparrows
singing loud and off-key.
Brown like cheek-stuffing squirrels
scurrying fast, tree to tree.

Brown like rustic pergolas
and benches crafted from wood.
Brown like hot, fresh-baked pastries
that—*sniff sniff*—smell good.

I look up. I look down.
I'm searching to see something

**wonderfully,**
**marvelously**
**brown**

—just like **me!**

**Brown** like big, busy beavers
building dams with large sticks.
Playful otters splish–splashing,
swimming fast, doing tricks.

**Brown** like cool river paddlers
in handmade cedar canoes.
Brown like two long-tailed thrashers
sing-singing the blues.

**Brown** like brave adventurers.
Giant redwoods stretched high.
Great horned owls hoo-hooing
with quiet wings when they fly.

Brown like moths, flit-flittering,
as they stir in the night.
Brown like ten tiny mice
hidden well in plain sight.

I look left. I look right.

I'm searching to see something

# wonderfully,
# marvelously
# brown

—just like me!

**Brown** like strong bighorn sheep
that climb high, leap, and run.
Like rare desert tortoises
that bask in the sun.

**Brown** like Grand Canyon walls,
mules and hikers on trails,
mountain lions with cubs,
flick-flicking their tails.

**Brown** like kayakers gliding.
Brown like boats tied to docks.
Piping plovers peep-peeping,
laying eggs among rocks.

**Brown** like creeping coyotes
that yip, howl, and bark.
Campers sipping hot cider
by the fire before dark.

I look over and under.
I'm searching to see something

## wonderfully,
## marvelously
## brown

—just like **me!**

**Brown** like a pelican
diving fast for a fish.
Like a mourning dove's wings
whistling loud when they swish.

**Brown** like grizzly bear cubs
wrestling, rolling, and romping.
Brown like moose with long legs.
Brown like mukluks stomp-stomping.

**Brown** like roadrunners sprinting,
leaving X marks as tracks.
Brown like mama opossums,
joeys gripping their backs.

**Brown** like ten-gallon hats.
Longhorns crowding a street.
Like folklórico dancers
stamp-stamping their feet.

I look near. I look far.

I'm searching to see something

# wonderfully,
# marvelously
# brown

—just like me!

**Brown** like loggerhead turtles.
Snorkelers swimming with flippers.
Brown like five-armed sea stars
waving suction-cup grippers.

**Brown** like stinging sea jellies,
frilly tentacles swaying.
Brown like porcupine fish
eating, hiding, and playing.

**Brown** like warm, breezy beaches.
Brown like toes in the sand.
Brown like castles with towers,
each one molded by hand.

**Brown** like piles of wet driftwood.
Brown like surfers on boards.
Ukulele bands strumming,
pick-picking four chords.

I look here. I look there.
I'm searching to see something

# wonderfully,
# marvelously
# brown

—just like **me!**

**Brown** like baked marranitos.
Champurrado in mugs.
Like the squeeze-squeezing arms
of Abuela's big hugs.

**Brown** like smooth satin bonnets.
Stuffies tucked into bed
while spectacular browns
whirl around in my head.

God made so many colors,
each a beautiful hue.

Still, I'm glad He used **brown**
when He made **me** and **you.**